Dear Parent:

Congratulations! Your child the first steps on an exciting journey. The destination? Independent reading!

STEP INTO READING® will help your child get there. The program offers five steps to reading success. Each step includes fun stories and colorful art. There are also Step into Reading Sticker Books, Step into Reading Math Readers, Step into Reading Write-In Readers, Step into Reading Phonics Readers, and Step into Reading Phonics First Steps! Boxed Sets—a complete literacy program with something for every child.

Learning to Read, Step by Step!

Ready to Read Preschool–Kindergarten
• big type and easy words • rhyme and rhythm • picture clues
For children who know the alphabet and are eager to begin reading.

Reading with Help Preschool–Grade 1
• basic vocabulary • short sentences • simple stories
For children who recognize familiar words and sound out new words with help.

Reading on Your Own Grades 1–3
• engaging characters • easy-to-follow plots • popular topics
For children who are ready to read on their own.

Reading Paragraphs Grades 2–3
• challenging vocabulary • short paragraphs • exciting stories
For newly independent readers who read simple sentences with confidence.

Ready for Chapters Grades 2–4
• chapters • longer paragraphs • full-color art
For children who want to take the plunge into chapter books but still like colorful pictures.

STEP INTO READING® is designed to give every child a successful reading experience. The grade levels are only guides. Children can progress through the steps at their own speed, developing confidence in their reading, no matter what their grade.

Remember, a lifetime love of reading starts with a single step!

For Ramona, who loves all creatures
cute and cuddly

www.stepintoreading.com

www.randomhouse.com/kids/disney

Educators and librarians, for a variety of teaching tools, visit us at www.randomhouse.com/teachers

Library of Congress Cataloging-in-Publication Data
Jordan, Apple.
The koala king / by Apple Jordan; illustrated by the Disney Storybook Artists.
p. cm. — (Step into reading. Step 2 book)
ISBN: 0-7364-2303-6 (trade)
ISBN: 0-7364-8038-2 (lib. bdg.)
PZ7.J755Koa 2006
2005022522

Printed in the United States of America   10 9 8 7 6 5 4 3 2 1

STEP INTO READING, RANDOM HOUSE, and the Random House colophon are registered trademarks of Random House, Inc.

STEP INTO READING

DISNEY'S THE WILD

THE KOALA KING

by Apple Jordan

illustrated by the Disney Storybook Artists

Random House 🏠 New York

Nigel is a koala.

He lives in the zoo.

Toy koalas are cuddly.

But Nigel is not a toy.

He does not like

being cuddly.

He wants to be

big and strong.

Samson is a lion.

He <u>is</u> big and strong.

He tells his son, Ryan,

about the Wild.

One day,
Ryan was taken
to the Wild.

Samson had to get
Ryan back.

Nigel and his friends
wanted to go, too.
Samson told them
it would not be safe.
But they had to help.

The gang set sail
for the Wild.
They had to find Ryan.

The trip was
long and hard.
Nigel was hot.
Nigel was hungry.

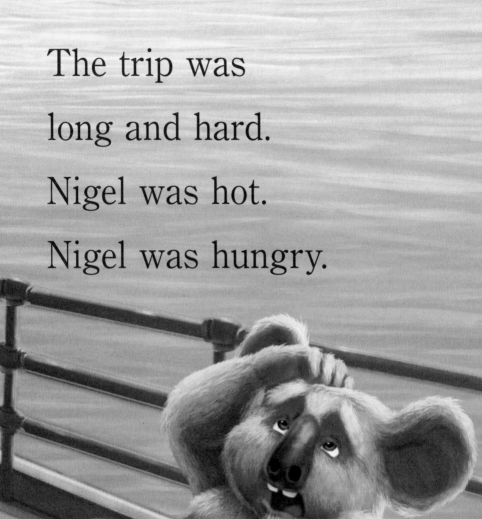

Nigel was fed up.
He jumped
off the boat.

Nigel hit land.
They reached
the Wild at last!

The gang went
in search of Ryan.
But Nigel fell behind.
He was on his own.

17

Nigel met a pack
of beasts
in the Wild.

They bowed
down to him.
They were happy
to see him.

Long ago
a toy koala
had fallen
from the sky.

The toy saved the beasts
from hungry lions.
It was a sign
that one day
the beasts would rule.

Now a real koala
had come to the beasts.
The beasts thought
Nigel would help
them rule the Wild.

They made him
their king.
Nigel liked being king.

The beasts found some
of Nigel's friends.
They even found Ryan!

But the beasts wanted
to cook his friends.
Nigel had to think fast.

Samson showed up
just in time!
Nigel needed help.
They made a plan
to save the gang.

Nigel tricked
the beasts.
He faked a fight
with Samson.

It worked!
The gang got away.
They even made
some new friends.
Nigel saved the day!

The friends headed
home at last.

Nigel threw
the cuddly toy away
once and for all.
He proved that he was
one big strong koala.